W9-CAB-634

SECOND–CHANCE
SOCCER

BY JAKE MADDOX

text by
Thomas Kingsley Troupe

STONE ARCH BOOKS
a capstone imprint

Jake Maddox JV books are published by Stone Arch Books
A Capstone Imprint
1710 Roe Crest Drive
North Mankato, Minnesota 56003
www.capstonepub.com

Library of Congress Cataloging-in-Publication Data

Maddox, Jake, author.
  Second-chance soccer / by Jake Maddox ; text by Thomas Kingsley Troupe ; illustrated by
Mike Ray.
     pages cm. -- (Jake Maddox JV)
  Summary: Sixth-grader Alex really wants to make his middle school soccer team this year,
but Jake, the class bully, keeps taunting him with his past failures — until Errol, a new
student from Scotland, teaches him the importance of practice and teamwork.
  ISBN 978-1-4342-9154-7 (library binding) -- ISBN 978-1-4342-9158-5 (pbk.)-- ISBN 978-1-4965-
0065-6 (eBook PDF)
1. Soccer stories. 2. Bullying--Juvenile fiction. 3. Friendship--Juvenile fiction. 4. Teamwork
(Sports)--Juvenile fiction. 5. Middle schools--Juvenile fiction. [1. Soccer--Fiction. 2. Bullying--
Fiction. 3. Friendship--Fiction. 4. Teamwork (Sports)--Fiction. 5. Middle schools--Fiction. 6.
Schools--Fiction.] I. Troupe, Thomas Kingsley, author. II. Ray, Mike (Illustrator), illustrator.
III. Title.

 PZ7.M25643Se 2014
 813.6--dc23

                          2013047038

Art Director: Heather Kindseth
Designer: Veronica Scott
Production Specialist: Jennifer Walker

Photo Credits:
Shutterstock: macknimal, chapter openings, Wendy Nero, cover, 1
Design Elements: Shutterstock

Printed in China by Nordica
0414/CA21400620
032014   008095NORDF14

TABLE OF CONTENTS

CHAPTER I

COACH PALMER

Alex Carver sat up straight in his desk chair when he heard footsteps outside the door to his classroom. His teacher, Mr. Blythe, had mentioned that Coach Palmer was planning to stop by to talk to the class today. It was something the soccer coach did every year — issue a personal invite to the boys of Longhorn Junior High School to join the state's best varsity soccer team, the Longhorn Lightning.

Alex had wanted to play on the Longhorn Lightning for as long as he could remember. Every single year, the Lightning crushed the competition and took home the state trophy. The team had the opportunity to travel around the state, be featured on the local news, and play in a stadium filled with cheering fans.

It was Alex's dream to be part of the winning team. But that dream had died a painful death at last year's tryouts when he'd managed to completely embarrass himself. Instead of playing for the Lightning, he'd ended up stuck on the intramural soccer team — where anyone not good enough for the Lightning got assigned.

Just then, there was a loud knock at the classroom door. It opened, and Coach Palmer stuck his head inside.

"All right, everyone," Mr. Blythe said, waving the soccer coach into the classroom. "Please put away your assignments for now. We're going to give Coach Palmer our undivided attention for a few moments."

Coach Palmer made his way up to the front of the classroom. He was an older man with gray hair cut so short he looked like he could be in the military. His stern face and eyebrows were constantly furrowed, as if everything he saw made him mad. Today, like most other days, his mouth was clamped in a tight line, only opening when he had something important to say.

To Alex, Coach Palmer was like a superhero. Back when he'd played, Coach Palmer had been insanely talented on the field. He'd played professional soccer for years until a knee injury had forced him to retire.

After his retirement, Coach Palmer had moved back to Longhorn to lead the soccer team. Thanks to his skill and knowledge of the game, the Lightning had been crowned state champions nine years in a row.

"All right, kids," Coach Palmer said. He paced back and forth like an army general in front of the first row of seats. "I think you all know why I'm here, so I'll keep this short and to the point. We have Lightning soccer season ahead of us, and I want the school's best players to join us on the field this year."

Alex resisted the urge to raise his hand and shout, *That's me! I'll join! I'm in!*

"Seventh and eighth graders make up our varsity team — plus a few sixth graders if they're lucky," the coach continued. "We had about half of our championship team move up to high school this year, so we have some serious shoes to fill."

The coach looked around the room, staring at each and every one of the boys. He seemed to be trying to sense which ones might be worthy additions to the Lightning team.

"Don't you mean cleats?" Mr. Blythe interrupted with a little laugh. "Cleats to fill?"

Oh, Mr. Blythe, Alex thought, grimacing at his teacher's bad joke. *Please don't.*

When the uncomfortable silence had passed, Coach Palmer held up a thick stack of yellow papers. They were bright and bold, just like lightning.

Alex sat up a little straighter in his chair. He knew what those papers were from last year — the sign-up sheets for the soccer team tryouts.

"Tryouts will be held one month from Saturday," Coach Palmer announced. "That gives you boys plenty of time to sharpen your skills and bring the best to my field."

Coach Palmer paused for a moment. He looked around the room at the faces staring back him.

"Longhorn has a deep tradition of championship soccer to uphold," the coach told the class. "I know there are plenty of good players who want to help us keep the Lightning on top. But I don't want just good. I want the best."

No one said anything. It seemed like everyone in the room was afraid to even breathe.

"Let's seem some hands, Lightning hopefuls," Coach Palmer said, glancing around the classroom once again.

A few rows up, Jake Wallace raised his hand right away, just like Alex knew he would. Jake had been on the team last year and was one of the few sixth graders who'd been allowed to play.

Coach nodded and winked at him. "Attaboy, Jake," he said. "It'll be great to have you back on the field."

A few of Jake's friends raised their hands, too, and Coach nodded his approval. He passed the fliers their way.

Alex glanced over at Jake's crew. *They probably won't even have to try out*, he thought. *Coach Palmer likes them already.*

Alex's heart thumped heavily in his chest as the coach passed fliers to a couple other guys brave enough to ask for one. He looked around the classroom once more.

"Anyone else?" Coach asked. He straightened his fliers like he was getting ready to move to another classroom.

Alex wanted so badly to raise his hand. *Do it*, he thought. *What's the holdup? What are you waiting for?*

But then he remembered last year's tryouts again. Alex had been so nervous he'd tripped over his own feet the entire time. He'd barely been able to keep up with the other players when it came to running laps or controlling the ball. He hadn't stood a chance of making the team.

Alex shook his head. As much as he wanted to, he couldn't make himself do it. *What if I screw up again?* he thought.

"Okay then," Coach Palmer said. "I'll see you boys in a month."

Alex saw his chance start to slip away. Before he could stop himself, he stood up, almost knocking over his desk chair.

"Coach!" Alex called out. "Wait! Sorry. I'll take one of those."

Coach Palmer turned stared at Alex with one of his eyebrows raised. "You sure about this?" he asked. The coach held up a single flyer up. "You didn't speak up when I asked before."

Alex felt his heart stop for a second. Sweat beaded on his forehead. *Does he remember me from last year?* he wondered.

"Yeah . . . I mean, I'm sure," he finally managed to get out.

Coach Palmer nodded. "Okay," he said. He walked over to Alex and delivered the yellow piece of paper to him. "I'll see you on the field in a month, Alex."

He does remember me! Alex realized. He could feel every eye in the classroom on him as he took the piece of paper. Some girls in the back whispered. He heard Jake snort. Even Mr. Blythe adjusted his glasses to get a better look.

"Sounds good," Alex said. He hoped his voice didn't sound little and squeaky. "Thanks, Coach."

Coach Palmer nodded at him, and then, without another word, he turned around and walked out of the classroom.

CHAPTER 2

WHAT DID YOU SAY?

As soon as the lunch bell rang, Alex stood up from his desk. He carefully folded the soccer tryout sheet in half and slipped it into his math book to make sure he didn't lose it.

As Alex filed out of the classroom and into the busy hallway, he heard Jake and his friends mumbling nearby. He just hoped they weren't talking about him.

Alex got to his locker and dropped his book inside. When he turned around, Jake, Cole Bergman, and Jesse Fillion were standing together in a group watching him. Alex pretended not to see them and closed his locker.

"You actually think you'll do better this year, Carver?" Jake asked with a sneer. His arms were folded over his chest.

Alex sighed. He had no choice but to turn and face them. "I guess we'll see," he said with a shrug. He looked around for his friends Tim or Joe, but he didn't see either of them.

Probably already at the lunch table, Alex thought. *Thanks, guys.*

"You stunk up the field last year," Cole said. "Tripping over your own feet like you'd just learned how to walk."

Jake jumped right in. "The intramural team is where losers like you should keep playing," he said. "Remind me, were you named one of the four intramural MVPs last year?"

"No," Alex forced himself to say. He gripped the top of his brown paper lunch bag tightly.

"Did your team win the intramural championship? Refresh my memory, Carver," Jake said with a sneer.

"No," Alex said quietly.

Jake's sidekicks laughed meanly. A couple girls from their class slowed down to watch.

"So if Coach wants the best for his team, and you were barely good enough to be on the intramural team, how do you think you stand a chance of playing for the Lightning?" Jake asked.

Alex was silent a moment, not sure what to say. As he was about to respond, a boy he'd never seen before pushed his way in between Alex and Jake.

"Beggin' your pardon, fellys," the boy said. "A dinnae whare —"

"Whoa, whoa," Jake interrupted. "What language are you speaking?"

The boy looked at Jake and his friends. "English, last I knew," the boy said. He stared Jake right in the eyes. Neither boy said a word.

Finally Jake frowned and looked away. "C'mon, guys," he said. "Looks like these two losers need some alone time."

Jake and the other boys smirked at Alex and the newcomer as they headed down the hall.

When they were out of sight, Alex let out a deep breath and shook his head. *I knew the competition to play on the Lightning was intense*, he thought, *but I didn't think it'd start until the tryouts at least.*

"You all right?" the boy asked.

"I'm fine," Alex said. "Aren't you Arrow? The new guy from Scotland or someplace?"

"Errol," the boy corrected. "Errol McKenzie. I'm chuffed to know ya."

"Chuffed?" Alex repeated. "What's that mean?"

"Eh, sorry," Errol said, shaking his head. "Glad. Mighty glad to meet you."

Alex nodded. "Yeah, you too. You might want to avoid saying things like chuffed," he said. "I think your accent is cool, but people here might not understand you."

Errol nodded. "Fair enough," he said. "Where does a felly eat roond here?"

Alex walked with Errol and showed him the way to the lunchroom. When they got there, Errol thanked him and ran over to the end of the hot lunch line.

Alex turned and looked for his friends. He caught sight of them at their usual lunch table.

"Hey, there he is," Tim Mathews called as Alex approached. He and Alex's other best friend, Joe Lamond, were already well into eating their lunches.

"Yeah, here I am," Alex confirmed, tossing his lunch onto the table. "Thanks for waiting, guys."

Joe was too busy eating a cold burrito to respond. He just shrugged.

Alex tore open his lunch and pulled his sandwich out of the bag. He glanced back over his shoulder to keep an eye on Jake and his gang carefully.

"Did Coach Palmer stop by your class too, Alex?" Tim asked.

"Yeah," Alex said, nodding.

"And?" Tim prodded him. "Are you going to try out again?"

"Sure," Alex said, trying to sound more confident than he felt. "I mean, why not? If I don't make it again this year, I'll play on the intramural team again."

Tim smirked. "Well, I'll be honest," he said. "I kind of hope you don't make it. We could use you on the field again this year."

Alex rolled his eyes. "Thanks, Tim," he said. "Real nice of you."

Tim put his hands up. "What? I'm just being honest," he said.

Joe wiped his mouth with the back of his hand. "Not real supportive, Tim," he muttered.

"So, I'm selfish," Tim said with a shrug. "So what? I'd rather have him on our team. We didn't do too badly last year."

"We got third place," Alex said between bites.

"Yeah," Tim said. "Third place is pretty good!"

Joe rolled his eyes. "There were only four intramural teams," he said. "And one of the games we won by forfeit because the other team didn't have enough players."

"Ah, details," Tim said with a laugh. "I'm just kidding, Alex. You'll do okay in the tryouts. You got a lot better last season."

Alex tried to smile. *That's the problem*, he thought. *Okay and better isn't good enough. Coach says I have to be the best.*

CHAPTER 3

FRONT-YARD FOES

After school that afternoon, Alex rode his bike home. He parked in the garage and glanced around at all the junk they had piled up. His parents had yet to drag out anything for the yard that season.

Alex started digging through a few boxes full of inflatable pool toys for his younger brothers, a collection of yard games, and a deflated beach ball. After a few moments, he found what he was looking for.

"Gotcha," Alex whispered, spotting his soccer ball hidden beneath a rack of garden tools and camping gear.

Alex reached down between the storage bins and wheelbarrow and pulled the ball free. He hadn't used it since his horrible experience at tryouts the previous season. At the time, he couldn't have cared less about finding it again.

Luckily, the soccer ball was in pretty decent shape, but it needed some air. Alex grabbed the pump and filled the ball up.

Finding the soccer net was much easier. His mom had twisted a few bicycle hooks into the wooden studs along the inside of the garage and hung the net up there.

With a grunt, Alex lifted the net free and headed for the front yard. He set the net down on the far edge of the grass. Just kicking the ball into an open net wouldn't do much in the way of practice, but he needed to start somewhere.

First Alex worked on dribbling the ball across the yard. It had been a while since he'd done it, but it came back to him. He over-bumped it and sent it shooting out sideways toward the house a few times. Another time, it fell down into one of the basement window wells.

When he grew tired of footwork, Alex set up to practice a penalty kick. There wasn't a wall of defenders to kick around, but he took his best shot.

The soccer ball zipped toward the net but his aim was off. The ball hit the left post and bounced out into the street. Alex watched it bounce twice and roll to a stop in front of a parked car.

"Looks like I was wrong about you, Carver!" a voice shouted from down the street.

Alex groaned. He didn't need to look to see who it was. As if seeing Jake at school wasn't bad enough, he and Alex also lived on the same block.

"Great," Alex muttered, heading after the ball. Who knew what Jake would do if he got to it first?

"I might as well not even try out," Jake shouted. He was riding on his bike alongside Jesse. "You've got my position all locked down!"

Alex wanted to ignore Jake. He kept hoping the other boy would get bored enough to leave him alone, but so far it hadn't happened.

Alex had had enough. "What's your problem with me, man?" he snapped. "Seriously?"

Jake and Jesse slowed their bikes to a stop near Alex. "It's simple, Carver," Jake said. "We don't need bad players on our team. You can barely handle the ball, and you take dumb shots."

"I'm not that bad," Alex said, shaking his head.

"Yeah, well, you're not that good, either," Jake snapped. "Just save us all the trouble, and stay on the intramural team with your little buddies where you belong. Leave the real soccer to real players."

"Real soccer?" Alex muttered. "We played as hard as you guys did last year. There's only so much room on the Lightning, Jake."

"Exactly," Jake said. "Only room for the best."

"Get over yourself," Alex said. He walked back to his house with his soccer ball to practice more.

"That's right, Carver," Jake taunted him. "Walk away. Quit while you're behind. You'll never wear a Lightning jersey! Not in this lifetime!"

As Jake and Jesse rode off, Alex heard them laughing.

"Ya can't let 'em talk to you like that, mate," another familiar voice said.

Man, Alex thought. *Can't a guy practice in private?*

He turned to see Errol standing on the sidewalk. The other boy had his backpack slung over his shoulder, and his arms were crossed in front of his body.

Alex shrugged and shook his head. "Yeah, well, it's just talk."

"Back in Scotland we would've given them a love tap to the nose," Errol said. "So you're a fitba player, then?"

"Fitba?" Alex repeated. "Oh, you mean football? No, I play soccer."

"Eh, it's football where I come from," Errol said. "I mean, the game is played with your feet, right? And there's a ball involved and all."

Alex shrugged again. "Yeah, I guess that makes sense. Do you play soccer?"

Errol shook his head. "Not anymore I don't," he said. "It's a wee bit different here for my tastes. Besides, I wouldn't care to play on a team with those blokes." He nodded toward the end of the street where Jake and Jesse had disappeared.

"Were you any good when you did play?" Alex asked. He bounced the ball on his knee.

"I booted a fair game," Errol said with a smile. "And I could show ya a few things if it suited ya."

Alex considered Errol's offer. Sure, he wanted to learn a few things, especially if Errol was a decent "footballer" like he claimed. But he didn't know how someone his own age could coach him.

"Well, I appreciate the offer," Alex said, "but I thought you didn't even like soccer anymore."

"I never stopped loving the game," Errol said. "Just needed a break from it. After all, I've been playing football since I was a wee bairn."

"A what?" Alex asked.

Errol smacked his head. "Apologies," he said. "A child. That's what we say back home. Me dad is radge about the game. Had me playing young."

Alex still had a hard time deciphering Errol's heavy accent. "So . . . he was angry about soccer?" he asked.

Errol shrugged. "Not really angry, more like crazy about it. Like he was a big fan? He used to get in fights with fans in the other team's colors."

Alex whistled. He liked certain sports teams, and it was fun to be competitive, but to fight someone wearing another team's jersey? It sounded like Errol's dad was crazy about soccer.

It also sounded like Errol was the perfect guy to get Alex ready for tryouts. "Okay," he agreed. "Let's do it."

CHAPTER 4

PARK PRACTICE

The first thing Alex and Errol did was head to a park several blocks from Alex's house. The park was big and grassy with a large open area where families could come to picnic when it was nice.

"Why couldn't we just stay and practice in my yard?" Alex asked as they set up the soccer net.

"You've got those choobs roond the block hanging about," Errol said. "The last thing you need while practicin' is to have to answer to the likes of them."

Choobs, Alex thought and smiled. He guessed it meant "jerks."

"Aye, this'll do much better than your yard," Errol said. "Ya can't train in a small space like that. Ya need the space to stretch your legs. Half of fitba is the running."

Alex nodded. He remembered his tryouts for the Lightning last year. He'd been so winded from running back and forth across the field that he'd done terribly in the tryout scrimmage.

Together Alex and Errol estimated the size of a soccer field and placed sticks in each corner. When they had the space all staked out, they started running. The run was easy at first, but after four laps, Alex wondered if Errol was just playing a mean joke on him.

"Okay," Alex said, struggling for breath. "I know I need to get used to running, but really? Aren't we going to even use the soccer ball?"

Errol slowed to a stop. "Of course," he said with a smile. "How else would we practice? Boot it here, would ya?"

Alex kicked the ball to Errol and watched his Scottish mentor do a bit of dribbling. He moved the ball back and forth, stopped it quickly, did a roll over, and continued. Errol was incredibly nimble, and Alex watched him fake a pass, keeping easy control of the ball the whole time.

"Wow," Alex said. He raised his eyebrows. "You're really fast."

Errol kicked the ball over, and Alex trapped it with his feet. It was tougher to do without his cleats, but he stopped it well enough.

Sensing that Errol wanted to see what he could do, Alex started dribbling down the field. He tapped the ball back and forth and did a roll back. But as he turned and ran back toward Errol, the ball got away from him. Before he could snap it up, Errol was on it.

"Here's one thing that might set you straight," Errol said. "Your stance is all wonky. You're standing straight up."

"Really?" Alex said. He didn't think that would matter much, but as he watched Errol, he noticed the other boy bent forward slightly while he worked the ball.

"Bending your back a bit keeps you centered and on top of the ball," Errol explained. He passed the ball over to Alex.

Alex bent forward a little, mimicking Errol's pose, and immediately felt the difference. He moved the ball between his feet, mixing it up with roll overs and outside taps. It was much easier to control the ball this way.

"Four more times roond with the ball," Errol said. "If you knock it loose, I'll scoop it up and get it back to ya. Let's get all the way roond once with no slipups."

"Isn't that a little tough to do?" Alex said, feeling worried.

"It is if you don't work on it, mate," Errol said. "Let's start."

Alex made his way around the field, concentrating on keeping the ball under control. The first lap was the toughest; the ball got away from Alex more times than he cared to count. But with each lap it got a little bit easier. On the fourth time around, the ball only came loose once, right at the end.

"Seriously?" Alex shouted. "I was so close!"

"You did well, Al," Errol said. "Honest."

But Alex wasn't convinced. He wanted to get all the way around without any mistakes. "Let's go again," he said. "This time it'll be perfect."

"Yeah," Errol replied with a smile. "Who needs a warm dinner anyway, right?"

CHAPTER 5

JUST FOR KICKS

Alex and Errol practiced every night after school for the next two weeks. They focused on Alex's footwork, his stamina, and his passing skills. Before long, thanks to all the running Errol made him do, Alex was hardly winded when he finished running laps around their makeshift field.

"What spot on the team are ya wantin'?" Errol asked one night as they finished warming up. "You know, when the coach picks ya?"

Alex laughed. Errol seemed to be convinced that Alex would make the team, even if Alex wasn't so sure himself.

"I'd like to be a midfielder or a forward," Alex admitted. "But I'm guessing I'll end up as a defender . . . if I make the team at all, that is."

Errol titled his head to the side and studied Alex. "Ye say defender like it's a bad position, Al. Don't ye know that the defenders are the blokes who save the match most times?"

Alex shrugged. "Yeah, I guess," he said. "I'd just be happy to be on the team. I know I'd never want to be goalie. I tried that last year on the intramural team. Not for me."

Errol nodded. "Fair enough," he replied. "I'm not much in the box either. Plus, I like to run. I was a pretty radge midfielder back home."

Alex smiled. Listening to Errol talk about soccer in his cool Scottish accent was always entertaining.

"So here's the score," Errol said, kicking the ball up and juggling it with his knees. "You and I are going to play one-on-one football today."

Alex looked at the huge field. "Seriously? We don't have any goalies or anything. How's that going to work?"

"Let's see if you can get the ball away from me before you worry about that, Al," Errol said with a sly grin. "You up for a match?" He tossed the ball up in the air toward Alex.

Instead of answering, Alex headed the ball in midair and knocked it downfield. He didn't wait for Errol to move before he took off after it. Knowing how good his new friend was, Alex had a feeling his time with the ball would be short-lived.

"You'd better run, mate," Errol shouted down the field after him.

Alex heard Errol's cleats pounding behind him. He kicked the ball farther toward his imaginary goal and sprinted after it. Errol wasn't far behind.

As Alex got closer to the ball, he wound up to kick the ball into the imaginary goal. Suddenly, though, he saw a blur out of the corner of his eye as Errol raced past him. Just as Alex booted the ball, Errol turned and used his body to block the shot.

"Defense!" Errol hollered, taking control of the ball. "You can't win a match without your defenders, Al."

"Show-off!" Alex yelled, but he was laughing.

In no time, Errol was dribbling the ball back down the field in the other direction. "Turn on the gas!" he shouted. "Give us some speed, will ya?"

Alex dug deep down for more energy and forced his legs to move faster. He sprinted after Errol and caught up quickly.

Alex watched the ball carefully as they moved downfield. Errol dribbled it back and forth, did a roll-over move, and attempted a fake.

Alex saw his opportunity. "Gotcha," he muttered, taking a swipe at the trapped ball. He knocked it loose and punted it back down the field toward the imaginary goal.

"Good eye, Al," Errol said. He clapped as he chased after Alex again. "Maybe there's hope for you yet!"

Alex dribbled back to the midline and faked to the left. Errol fell for it, shifting left, and Alex quickly juked to the right. Using his right foot, Alex did a roll over and then popped the ball up into the air with his left.

Before Errol could recover, Alex headed the ball hard, knocking it farther downfield. *Now's my chance*, he thought.

Both boys ran with everything they had as the ball bounced closer and closer to the invisible goal.

"Ya got wheels on ye, Al," Errol shouted. "But not fast enough, are ye?"

"I'm surprised your mouth doesn't slow you down," Alex shouted back and laughed. "Only Jake talks more trash than you!"

Errol beat Alex to the ball by half a step, but it was enough. He trapped the ball, turned, and did a push-pull, pulling the ball back and then knocking it forward. Alex lunged at the wrong moment, and Errol turned and blazed past him.

Alex groaned as he watched Errol tear back down the field. *Stupid!* he thought. *I'm falling for the most basic fake-outs ever!*

Errol shouted something to him from up ahead, but Alex couldn't make it out. He dashed after him, knowing he couldn't just give in and let Errol have a free shot on his goal. Even though he was getting frustrated and wanted to quit, he wasn't going to.

I want to play on the Lightning, after all, Alex thought.

Alex ran with everything he had, but Errol was too close to the net. There was no way he'd be able to stop him from shooting on his empty goal. Even so, he gave it his all.

As he watched Errol wind up to kick it, Alex dove in front of his friend. But he was a moment too late. The ball sailed past him, flying through the spot where the net should've been.

As he hit the damp grass, Alex felt the air rush from his lungs. He rolled onto his back and looked up at the sky. A moment later, Errol's smiling face towered above his.

"Ye got wheels, Al," Errol said, extending his hand to pull him up. "I'll give ye that."

CHAPTER 6

TEAM EFFORT

Errol and Alex continued to play one-on-one nearly every afternoon. And even though Errol still beat him on a regular basis, Alex could tell he was playing better each time. He'd learned new moves and could swear he was getting faster.

But even with all those improvements, Alex still wasn't convinced he was good enough to make the Lightning. And there was only one week left until tryouts.

"It's fun playing against you, Errol," Alex said one afternoon. He'd lost to Errol again, but at least this time it was only by a few points. "But it's much different from playing with a field full of players, you know?"

"Aye," Errol said. "But think of it this way, Al. You're getting prime time with the ball when it's just the two of us."

"I guess you're right," Alex said. But it still wasn't the same, and he wasn't sure what else they could do. It wasn't like there were any teams he could practice with.

Or were there?

"Wait a second," Alex said. "I bet I could get some of the intramural guys to come play."

Errol scratched his head. "Ya think they'd fancy a match?"

Alex shrugged. "There's only one way to find out," he said.

That night, Alex made a bunch of calls. He used the team roster from his intramural season the year before. Tim and Joe were happy to play and offered to call a few guys from the other teams, too. They planned to meet Saturday morning at the school — that way they wouldn't have to pretend there were nets.

When Alex hung up, he scanned his list and did a quick head count. He'd found ten more guys to play, but there weren't enough for two whole teams. Alex called Errol to see if he could find a few people too.

"I don't have much here in the way of friends, Al," Errol admitted. "But we'll make do with the lads we have."

* * *

On Saturday morning, the group met on the soccer field at Longhorn Junior High. Alex greeted everyone and looked around for Errol. It didn't look like his new friend was there yet.

"So," Ty Winfield, a guy from the Lions intramural team, began, "you're really going to try out for the varsity team again, huh?"

"Might as well," Alex said, shrugging. "What's the worst that can happen? They tell me no?"

Ty nodded. "So what's the deal with this Scottish guy? Is he like your soccer tutor?" The other guys looked curious too.

"He's a really good player," Alex explained. "I swear, I've learned more from him in the past few weeks than I did all of last year playing on the intramural teams."

"Seems kind of weird that a guy our age thinks he can coach," Joe said. "And if he's so good, why isn't he trying out for the Lightning, too?"

Alex shrugged. "He says he's not into playing here in the States," he said. "I don't know. I think he'd give the Lightning starters from last year a serious run for their money. Errol's got some major skills."

Just then, Errol zipped along the end of the field on his bike. As he approached and hopped off of his bike, he smiled. "Looks like we got all of the town's football hooligans in one spot," he said. "You blokes ready to play?"

The other guys laughed and stretched.

"So what're you thinking for teams?" Alex asked. He counted. All twelve guys had shown up as promised. "Should we just go six on six?"

Errol shook his head. "Naw, I was thinking more like ten on two."

Alex laughed. "Seriously?" he said. "We've got an even number. I know it's not a real team, but we can make it work."

But Errol was firm. "Trust me on this," he said. "You and I will take on the lot of these guys. It'll force us to work on our passing game."

When Alex told the rest of the guys what their plan was, Ty laughed. "Are you serious?" he asked.

"Sure thing," Errol replied. "Kick us up and down the pitch if ya fancy."

The guys agreed, and before Alex knew it, he was playing the most uneven soccer match of his life. Errol left the goal empty, and whenever he got the ball, he made sure to boot it to Alex right away.

During one drive downfield, Alex found himself moving the ball well, past the two midfielders on the other team, until he was within shooting distance to the goal. But before he could take his shot, the other team's defenders surrounded him, blocking his view of the net.

"Back here, Al," Errol shouted.

Alex glanced over and saw Errol open near the sideline. He quickly trapped the ball and booted it with his instep in Errol's direction. The ball went straight to Errol's waiting cleats.

As the defenders dashed toward Errol, Alex ran closer to the net. He watched as Errol wound up and kicked. The ball flew out and around the wall of defenders in a nearly perfect bend. It landed with one bounce neatly at Alex's feet.

The goalie, a guy named Stephen, gasped. Taking advantage of his surprise, Alex wound up and kicked the ball, shooting it right past Stephen's arms and into the net.

"Get out of here!" Tim shouted as he ran toward their goal. "That was insane, man! There's no way —"

Alex fist-bumped Errol. "That's just one goal," he said. "We're just getting started, guys. Let's keep at it!"

They continued to play for another twenty minutes before Alex saw a familiar trio on bikes pull up along the sidelines. Jake and his friends had arrived.

CHAPTER 7

UNINVITED GUESTS

"Hey, don't let us interrupt this episode of Soccer: Dork Edition, Carver," Jake called. "What've we got here? All the rejects from last year's intramural teams?"

Cole and Jesse laughed at Jake's joke, and Alex just shook his head. Not only was Jake insulting Alex, now he was making fun of all of the other guys on the field, too.

For a guy who only has two friends to back him up, Jake sure has guts, Alex thought. *Nasty guts, but guts nonetheless.*

"Why don't you just get out of here, Jake?" Alex said, walking toward the front of the crowd. "We weren't bothering any of you. We're just practicing."

Jake put his hands up and mocked excitement. "Oooh," he said. "Practicing for your big tryout next week? You should just save your time and energy, Carver. There's no way you're getting on the team. Not the way you play. And not if I have anything to say about it."

Alex folded his arms across his chest. "You sure seem awfully worried about me making the cut, Jake," he said. "Otherwise, why bother giving me such a hard time about it?"

There were a few *oohs* from the rest of Alex's soccer pals. Jake seemed momentarily stung that Alex was fighting back. But it didn't take long for the other boy to snap back.

"I'm not worried," Jake sneered. "The day you make the team is the day I'd quit, anyway."

"Well, the intramural teams would be happy to have you, Jake," Ty called. "Maybe you could bring us water or something."

Jake laughed meanly, but both Cole and Jesse were starting to look a little uncomfortable. Especially since Jake seemed to be digging himself deeper and deeper into a hole.

How can either of them stand being around a guy who talks and acts like he does? Alex thought in disbelief.

"Like I'd ever think about playing on some no-talent, intramural team," Jake shouted. "No real athlete plays in those leagues!"

Alex was about to stick up for his friends and former teammates when Errol stepped forward. He held the soccer ball in the crook of his arm and stared Jake down.

"What're you looking at?" Jake snapped at him. He looked ready to hop off of his bike and take a swing at Errol.

"I'm looking at sad, wee little footballer," Errol said quickly in his thick accent. "I see a bloke who's about to wet his keks when he gets shown up next Saturday."

Jake looked confused. "What are you even saying?" he snapped. "Speak English, why don't you? No one can understand a thing you just said."

Errol pointed at Jake, and his face grew serious. "Oh, I think ye heard me just fine, friend," he said. "Every last word."

There was an awkward silence as Jake struggled to come up with a response. When he didn't have anything to say, he moved back toward his friends.

"Whatever," Jake muttered. "C'mon, guys. Let's go. We should leave these losers to their little playtime."

As Jake and his friends peddled away down the street, Alex walked over to Errol. The rest of the players followed.

"Dang," Alex said, clapping his friend on the back and laughing. "You were downright scary there, Errol. What did even you say to him? Wet his keks?"

"Ah, keks is what we call trousers back home in Scotland," Errol said with a laugh. "I dipped into me accent a bit, I guess. Happens sometimes when I get worked up."

Alex turned to face the rest of the players. "We should keep playing," he shouted. "What do you guys think?"

Tim shrugged. "I don't know, Alex," he said. "Why would you even want to play on their team? If the other players are anything like Jake, why bother?"

Alex thought about it. Tim had a point. *I did have fun playing on the intramural team last year*, he realized. He'd made some new friends, and while he wasn't as great a player, he'd learned quite a bit.

As he replayed the past year in his mind, Alex realized he didn't have a solid answer to give his friends.

"I'm not entirely sure," he admitted. "I used to just want to be part of the Lightning so I could be part of a winning team, you know? Play in a big stadium, be on TV, all that stuff."

The rest of the guys looked at him like they were hurt. "So the intramural team isn't good enough for you or something?" someone called angrily.

"Let me finish," Alex pleaded with them. "Now, I don't think any of that matters anymore. I had a blast playing with and against you guys all last year. But I think more than anything, I want to prove to myself that I can make it on the team. It's giving me something to work toward, you know what I mean?"

Tim nodded. "I guess that makes sense," he said. He grinned at Alex. "Besides, if you don't make it, you'll kick all kinds of butt in the intramural leagues after working this hard. It's a win-win."

Alex took a deep breath. "Yeah," he said. "I guess you're right."

As the guys started the game up again, Alex realized he was in a tough spot. He really liked playing soccer with the guys from last year, but none of them seemed excited about him leaving or even trying out, for that matter.

But I guess they're right, Alex thought. *Win-win. Even if I don't make it.*

"Heads up, Al!" Errol shouted as the ball rolled past him. Joe beat him to it, and the opposing team moved it downfield.

Alex snapped out of it and chased after the ball. He watched Errol sprint past and hop in front of the goal. But it was ten on one. The intramural crew moved the ball well and scored easily on Errol, tying up the match.

"Where's ya head, Al?" Errol asked. "You want to even up the teams?"

"Nope," Alex said. "Let's keep things like they are. I just have to work a little harder, that's all."

Errol smiled and threw his shoulder into Alex's. "That's the spirit," he said with a grin. "Now let's drive it down."

The intramural players stayed on the field well into the afternoon. And while Alex and Errol never ended up beating the other team in their uneven matches, they did manage to give the other ten players a real workout.

"I'm bummed we didn't win," Alex said to Errol once everyone else had said their goodbyes and headed home. "That would've been legendary."

"Ah, it served a purpose," Errol said. "You were moving the ball well around plenty of guys. They had to work hard to get it from ye."

Alex smiled. "You're right," he said, hopping on his bike. "But I'm beat. See you tomorrow?"

Errol nodded. "Aye," he said. "Tomorrow. It'll be our last practice before tryouts."

Alex knew if he wasn't ready for the tryouts by then, he never would be.

CHAPTER 8

TRYOUTS

On Saturday morning, Alex's stomach felt like it was a huge ball of nerves. He almost didn't want to eat the breakfast his mom made for him, but he knew he should. It would be hard to play on an empty stomach.

And I need all the energy I can get, Alex thought as he forced himself to eat a few bites of his scrambled eggs. He ate some of his toast and washed it down with a swallow of orange juice. Then he stood up from the table.

"I have to go, Mom," Alex said. "See you later."

His mom glanced over at his plate and shook her head when she saw how little he'd eaten. "I wish you'd eat a bit more, honey," she said. "It's not a good idea for you to do all that running around on a mostly empty stomach."

Alex nodded. "I know," he said. "But I need to get there. I'm nervous enough."

His mom hugged him and shooed him out the door. "You'll do great, Alex," she called as he ran out the back door and hopped on his bike. "And no matter what, we're proud of you!"

* * *

After he parked his bike and changed into his cleats, Alex headed out to the soccer field. A group of Longhorn Lightning hopefuls were already gathered around Coach Palmer.

Alex found a spot at the edge of the group and looked around. There had to be somewhere around thirty guys already standing there. Alex recognized a bunch of guys from last year's team, including Cole, Jesse, and of course, Jake.

Alex did his best to avoid Jake's gaze. Instead he looked out into the stands. There, standing along the fence near the bleachers, was Errol.

At least I'll have one person here who thinks I can do it, Alex thought.

"All right, boys, listen up," Coach Palmer said. He tugged his baseball cap down low over his eyes to shield them from the sun. "First of all, thank you for coming out today. Just seeing how many people we have here at tryouts makes me happy."

Coach Palmer glanced around at the faces watching him. "What doesn't make me happy is knowing that a good number of you won't make the team," he continued, shaking his head.

Alex felt his heart sink at the coach's words.

"That's just the reality of it," Coach Palmer said. "We only have so many spots, and not everyone can play with the Longhorn Lightning.

The good thing to know is, Longhorn has a great intramural league for those who want to keep playing soccer anyway."

There was a murmur in the crowd. As if on cue, Alex heard the voice he dreaded.

"Hey, Carver," Jake shouted. "He's talking about you!"

Alex ignored the other boy. There was no way he would let Jake into his head. Not today.

Coach Palmer gave Jake a stern look but didn't say anything. Instead, he talked about the drills they were going to run through.

When he was finished talking, he broke the crowd of boys into three different groups. Some went with Assistant Coach Friberg, others went with Coach Palmer, and Alex's group joined Assistant Coach Walters.

The groups all took turns rotating through different stations. First, Alex hustled the ball through a series of cones. Thanks to all his practice with Errol, his footwork was much better, and he kept control of the ball the entire time.

The assistant coach had them run the drill again and again. He made notes the entire time, looking for players with the fastest footwork and those who could move down the field quickly.

Alex marveled at the skill level of the more experienced players. Some of them made it look effortless to roll the ball between their feet, trap it, pull back, and keep going.

When the groups rotated, Alex passed Jake on his way to the next station.

"Still here, huh?" Jake taunted him. "Not too tired yet?"

"Barely breathing hard," Alex replied quietly. He kept moving and didn't give his opponent a chance to respond.

The next station had the players work on their defense skills. The boys rotated so that everyone had a turn as a defender, while the rest were positioned as midfielders and forwards at the halfway line.

When Alex took his two turns as defender, he did well. Jesse knocked a solid kick toward the goal, but Alex got in front of it, blocking the ball with his chest before faking right and booting it back up the field.

A moment later, another forward made a play for the goal. Alex watched his feet and saw the forward pause. He struck out with his left foot and knocked the ball loose. By the time the boy turned, Alex was on the ball and had kicked it away.

"Defense!" Errol shouted encouragingly from his position near the fence. He put a fist up and wore a huge smile on his face.

At the next station, players worked on their goal kicks, varying where the ball went within the net. Alex found that his time with Errol paid off. He was able to read the goalie and judge how quickly he'd be able to move to intercept the ball.

Coach Palmer watched as he scored on three of his four attempts.

With a nod, the coach looked down to jot something on his clipboard. When everyone had cycled through his turn, the coach put his whistle to his mouth and blew three sharp blasts.

"Gather around, guys," Coach said. "It's time for the final tryout challenge."

CHAPTER 9

A TEAM DIVIDED

Alex knew exactly what was coming next. Coach Palmer had done the same thing during last year's tryouts. He liked to take all of the boys who were trying out, split them in half, and have them play a massive game against each other.

Since it was tryouts, they didn't have to worry about having a regulation number of guys on the field. In fact, it was better when there were more people. Everyone had to work that much harder.

"How many do we have?" Coach Palmer asked.

The assistant coaches counted the boys standing around. Many of them were red-faced and sweaty from pushing themselves so hard.

"I counted twenty-nine," Assistant Coach Friberg replied.

"Me too," Assistant Coach Walters confirmed.

"Anyone feel like quitting?" Coach Palmer asked with a laugh. "Help us even up the teams?"

No one moved, although Alex saw a couple guys who probably considered it for a second.

"You need another?" a familiar voice called. "I'll jump in with the lot of ye. Even the score."

Alex looked up and saw Errol heading over.

"Great," Jake muttered. "Carver's marble-mouthed friend."

A couple guys laughed, but most of the others kept quiet. Alex wanted to badly to interject and stand up for his friend, but he stayed silent too.

"Hey, why not?" Coach Palmer said. "You've played soccer before?"

Errol nodded and squinted into the sun. "Aye," he said. "Football back home but played a fair bit of soccer here lately."

In no time at all, the teams had been divided up. And as luck would have it, Errol ended up on Alex's team.

Jake made sure to get a spot on the opposing team. When they counted off numbers one and two, he switched spots with another guy.

"Looks like you're up against the best, Carver," Jake snarled at him. "I'm going to have fun making you look bad."

Alex smiled and ignored Jake for what seemed like the millionth time that day. He refused to let him get into his head. No matter what.

I'm at tryouts to do my best and see if there's a spot for me on the Longhorn Lightning, Alex reminded himself. *Simple as that.*

"We'll play like we always do, Al," Errol said as they both tugged on their blue mesh practice jerseys. "Never mind what he's saying."

"I won't," Alex promised his friend. "I'm just here to play."

CHAPTER 10

SCRIMMAGE

Everyone took to the field, and at the whistle, the opposing team kicked off, knocking the ball deep into Alex's blue team territory. He stayed at midfield and watched as a cluster of defenders from his team swarmed to the ball.

Alex knew everyone wanted to show off to the coaches. *If I never get any chance at the ball, I probably won't make the cut*, he thought.

Errol swung around a forward from the opposing team, moving the ball easily around the group. On cue, Alex headed downfield, watching for his chance. Errol knocked the ball to him, but Jake was there to intercept it.

"Not today, Carver!" Jake shouted. "You have to be faster than that!"

Alex chased after Jake. He watched his feet and the ball carefully, waiting for Jake to make a mistake. But Jake's footwork was flawless. As one of the defenders approached, Jake faked to the left, did a roll over, and breezed past him.

He's good, Alex thought. He hated to admit it, but it was true.

Though plenty of his guys were open, Jake moved into scoring position, out-maneuvering everyone in his path.

Alex kept after him, but he knew it was no use. In a matter of moments, Jake launched the ball with a well-placed kick into the net.

While his teammates celebrated, Jake turned and ran toward Alex. "That's how soccer is played, Carver!" he shouted.

Alex took a deep breath and shook it off. He watched as the assistant coach brought the ball to midfield. It was still early in the game, but Alex was worried.

Did Coach Palmer see Jake completely outplay me? he thought. *What if he's already crossed me off the list?*

At the next kickoff, the ball went wide and to the right. Alex dashed toward it and got his feet on the ball. As other midfielders swarmed him, he trapped the ball, knocked it to a teammate, and made his way toward the goal.

After a few turnovers, the ball was back in the red team's possession. Alex got into the fray, stole it from Jesse, and made his way to the goal. But before he knew it, Jake was on him.

"What're you gonna do, Carver?" Jake said. "I'm about to make you look bad. Again!"

Alex moved the ball closer to the goal. He could hear the cleats pounding behind him. It seemed like everyone on the team, including Jake, was closing in on him. He pulled the ball to the left, found an opening, and took his shot.

The kick was spot on, but the ball sailed farther left than he'd planned. It hit the goal post and went wild, back into play.

"You totally stink, Carver!" Jake taunted him. "Quit while you're behind!"

Alex felt his ears burn with anger and embarrassment. He was mad at himself for missing the shot. He was mad that he'd looked dumb in front of the coaches. And he was furious that Jake wouldn't leave him alone.

I know I'm a better player than this, Alex thought. *He's getting to me and making me play like garbage!*

Alex forced himself to take a deep, calming breath. As much as he wanted to shout back, he didn't. He saw the ball moving back downfield and sprinted after it. Alex got into the thick of it, knocked the ball free from the red team, and kicked it to a teammate.

"Open!" Errol shouted from the sidelines.

The blue-team member kicked the ball in Errol's direction. The kick went high, and Errol jumped. He headed the ball before it went out of bounds. Alex quickly blasted past two defenders after it and got control of the ball again.

"Kick it in, Al! You've got it!" Errol urged.

Alex moved toward the goal and watched the goalie hunker down, waiting for the shot.

Suddenly another defender moved in, blocking Alex. Out of the corner of his eye, he saw one of his teammates. The other blue shirt was even closer and had a clear shot at the net. Alex passed the ball to him and watched as his teammate scored, tying up the game.

Well, I made him look good at least, Alex thought. *I just hope not taking the shot doesn't come back to hurt me.*

CHAPTER 11

SPORTSMANLIKE

The game went on, and Alex kept his head and heart in it. He didn't hesitate to move in and get at the ball. Jake hogged the ball and scored three more goals.

Toward the end of the match, the ball came loose and rolled just a few feet from Alex. He hustled after it, pulled it to him, and kept good control of it as he moved downfield. When he neared the goal, he took aim. With a strong kick, Alex knocked it in for the game's last goal.

The blue team cheered. Though it made Alex happy, it was too little too late for his team. The red team had trounced the blue team 8-3.

Is it too late for me, too? Alex wondered. The goal was nice, but he wasn't sure if it was enough to earn him a spot on the team. *After all, Coach doesn't want just good. He wants the best.*

As everyone stripped off their practice jerseys and tossed them in a pile, Errol came over and patted Alex on the back. "Ye did well, Al," Errol said. "Brought it to 'em in the end, mate."

"Hey, thanks," Alex said. "Not sure if it made any difference, though."

Errol shrugged. "We'll know soon enough."

Coach Palmer had the boys gather around and sit for a few minutes while the coaches talked amongst themselves. Alex knew from last year exactly what they were doing. The three coaches would compare notes and add the players they wanted for the Lightning to a final list.

There was no waiting or wondering if you made the team. Coach Palmer didn't believe in dragging it out. Alex would know in a matter of minutes if he was on the Lightning or going back to the intramural team.

Whatever the outcome, Alex felt good about his tryout. He was miles above the player he'd been last year. He just hoped it was enough.

Alex turned and saw Jake watching him from the other end of the crowd. A nasty smile twisted across Jake's lips, and he jerked his thumb to the side as if to say, *You're outta here!*

Coach Palmer walked back to the crowd of hopefuls, followed closely by the two assistant coaches. "This year's Lightning team is in my hand," the head coach said, holding up his clipboard. "If I call your name, I want you to come stand up here."

Alex felt his heart pounding in his chest. Coach Palmer didn't waste any time telling people how great they played or how bad he felt about not letting everyone on. It was all business from that moment forward.

As the first few names were called, Alex counted. Last year, Coach Palmer had chosen fifteen players to be on the Lightning. Alex didn't think that number would change.

Jake's name was called eighth. Alex sighed. He wasn't surprised. Jake was a good player, and the coaches would be foolish not to pick him. But even so, it stung a little bit as more and more names were called.

As the last two names were called, Alex's heart sank. He hadn't made it.

Coach Palmer held up the clipboard and nodded. "That's it, gentlemen," he said. "Standing before you is this year's Longhorn Lightning team. I want to say thank you to everyone who participated. There were a few players that were so close it was hard to choose."

Alex sighed, and he felt Errol put a hand on his shoulder. "Ye played yer best, Al," Errol said. "No cause to hang yer head about it."

Before Alex could respond, Jake was clapping and moving toward him. "Awful, awful effort, Carver," Jake called sarcastically. "Seriously. That was some of the worst playing I've seen in a long time. Why don't you and your weird-talking friend pack up and head back to the intramural squad? Later, losers!"

Alex sensed that Errol was ready to knock Jake's lights out. "No, don't," Alex whispered. "It's not worth it."

Instead of walking away, Alex forced himself to walk over to Jake. He held out his hand. "Congratulations, Jake," he said. "You're a great player, and you deserve to be on the team. Good luck this season."

Jake looked at Alex like he was crazy. With a sneer, he held his hand out. But when Alex tried to shake it, Jake pulled it away. "Are you kidding? I don't want to catch your awful soccer skills," he shouted. "They might rub off on me!"

Jake laughed and looked around for support, but none of the other guys made a sound. Jake grew quiet when he turned and saw Coach Palmer standing behind him.

"It seems I made a mistake," the coach said, staring Jake down. "I can't have someone like you on my team, Jake. Not this year."

Jake's face sank and slowly his friends moved away. "What?" he cried. "You can't do this to me. My name is on the list!"

"Not anymore it isn't," Coach Palmer said, keeping his tone even. "I won't have someone as unsportsmanlike as you on our team. I don't care how good you are."

Alex watched as Jake shook his head. He looked like he was ready to throw a fit.

"I'll be better, Coach," Jake shouted. "I promise. It was a joke, that's all."

Coach Palmer didn't respond. Instead, he turned to Alex. "You were next on our list, but we can only choose fifteen players each year," he said. "Seems we have room for one more. Still interested in being part of the Longhorn Lightning?"

Alex smiled so widely, he felt like his face was about to explode. "Absolutely," he said quickly.

"What? No!" Jake shouted. He kicked a nearby soccer ball across the field in anger. "That's unfair! You can't give away my spot! No, not to him! He's horrible, Coach! He was a terrible player in the intramural leagues!"

Coach Palmer threw down his clipboard. "I want you off of my field, Jake," he said, anger rising in his voice. He pointed to the gate leading to the parking lot. "Now!"

Alex watched as Jake stormed off. He was shouting the whole way, promising the coach that his parents would hear about what he'd done.

After a while, Alex couldn't hear him anymore. He couldn't hear a thing. He couldn't believe it. He was finally a member of the Longhorn Lightning.

* * *

Alex and Errol walked their bikes back home. Alex still couldn't believe that he'd actually made the team. And he knew he had one person in particular to thank for his second chance.

"Hey, Errol," Alex said as they got to his house, "I don't think I ever thanked you for everything. Helping me out and stuff."

"Ah," Errol said, waving away the thanks. "It wasn't me. It was all you, Al. You showed your true skills out there."

"Well, you were a huge part of it," Alex said. "I couldn't have done it without you."

Errol shrugged. "You're welcome, then."

Alex shook his head as if he still couldn't believe it. A question popped into his head just then. "You know, I never asked you why you helped me," Alex said. "I mean, you said you didn't even want to play soccer here."

Errol scratched his head and smiled. "You helped me back on me first day at school, didn't ya?" he said.

"What?" Alex didn't remember doing anything. He only remembered he could barely understand a thing Errol was saying. Back when he wasn't used to his accent.

"You showed me where the lunchroom was," Errol reminded him. "Everyone else looked at me like I was some sort of freak when I asked. Maybe it was the accent. But you always treated me like I was a friend."

Alex laughed. He'd completely forgotten about that. He had no idea that just being a decent guy would not only earn him a friend, but a spot on the Lightning after all.

Thomas Kingsley Troupe has written more than 30 children's books. His book *Legend of the Werewolf* (Picture Window Books, 2011) received a bronze medal for the Moonbeam Children's Book Award. Thomas lives in Woodbury, Minnesota with his wife and two young boys.

GLOSSARY

accent (AK-sent)—the way that you pronounce words

appreciate (uh-PREE-shee-ate)—to enjoy or value somebody or something

assignment (uh-SINE-muhnt)—a specific job that is given to somebody

competition (kom-puh-TISH-uhn)—a situation in which two or more people are trying to get the same thing

confident (KON-fuh-duhnt)— certain that things will happen the way that you want

decipher (di-SYE-fur)—to figure out something that is written in code or hard to understand

nimble (NIM-buhl)—able to move quickly and lightly

roster (ROS-ter)—a list of persons or groups, such as teammates and positions

DISCUSSION QUESTIONS

1. Talk about the ways that Errol was a good friend to Alex throughout this story. Did their friendship change at all from beginning to end?

2. Why do you think Jake was so rude to Alex throughout this story? Talk about some possible reasons.

3. Imagine you're a player on the intramural soccer team. Talk about how you would feel about Alex wanting to play for the Lightning.

WRITING PROMPTS

1. Pretend you're Errol. Write an e-mail to your family back home, telling them about your new school, friends, and the soccer team.

2. What do you think the best part of being exchange student would be? What do you think the hardest part would be? Write a paragraph about each.

3. Write about a time you had to work hard and practice in order to succeed. What did you do? How did you feel?

MORE ABOUT
SOCCER

No one knows for sure when soccer was invented, but there's evidence that people in **ANCIENT CHINA** played a similar game more than 2,000 years ago.

The **UNITED STATES** and **CANADA** are the only countries that use the term "soccer" to describe the sport. Other countries call it "football."

Soccer players run an average of **SIX MILES** during every game.

The **WORLD CUP** is the largest international soccer match in the world. It's held every four years with teams from 32 countries competing.

The **BRAZILIAN SOCCER TEAM** has won the World Cup five times — the most of any country.

More than one billion fans watch the **WORLD CUP** on television.

Considering that soccer is the most popular sport in the world, it's no surprise that there are so many fun facts guaranteed to impress your friends on and off the field.

The most soccer fans to watch a World Cup soccer game was 119,850 in BRAZIL in 1950.

The fewest number of fans to watch a World Cup soccer game was 300 in URUGUAY in 1930.

EUROPEAN TEAMS have reached the World Cup finals every year except for two — in 1930 and 1950.

INDIA withdrew from the World Cup in 1950 because they weren't allowed to play barefoot.

The largest soccer tournament ever held took place in BANGKOK in 1999. More than 35,000 fans competed.